Can little friends be great friends?

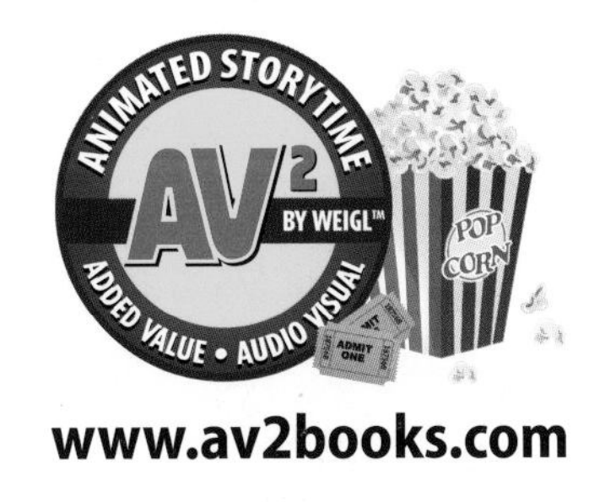

www.av2books.com

Go to www.av2books.com, and enter this book's unique code.

BOOK CODE

H874671

AV² by Weigl brings you media enhanced books that support active learning.

Published by AV² by Weigl
350 5th Avenue, 59th Floor New York, NY 10118

Library of Congress Control Number: 2013943511

ISBN 978-1-62127-919-8 (Hardcover)
ISBN 978-1-48960-133-9 (Multi-user eBook)

Senior Editor: Heather Kissock
Project Coordinator: Alexis Roumanis
Art Director: Terry Paulhus

Printed in the United States in North Mankato, Minnesota
1 2 3 4 5 6 7 8 9 0 17 16 15 14 13

052013
WEP300513

FABLE SYNOPSIS

For thousands of years, parents and teachers have used memorable stories called fables to teach simple moral lessons to children.

In the Aesop's Fables by AV² series, classic fables are given a lighthearted twist. These familiar tales are performed by a troupe of animal players whose endearing personalities bring the stories to life.

In *The Lion and the Mouse*, Aesop and his troupe teach their audience that even the toughest creatures sometimes need a helping hand, and that help may come from unexpected places. They learn that even little friends can be great friends.

This AV² media enhanced book comes alive with...

Animated Video
Watch a custom animated movie.

Try This!
Complete activities and hands-on experiments.

Key Words
Study vocabulary, and complete a matching word activity.

Quiz
Test your knowledge.

Can little friends be great friends?

AV² Storytime Navigation

Aesop

I am the leader of Aesop's Theater, a screenwriter, and an actor.
I can be hot-tempered, but I am also soft and warm-hearted.

Libbit

I am an actor and a prop man.
I think I should have been a lion, but I was born a rabbit.

Presy

I am the manager of Aesop's Theater.
I am also the narrator of the plays.

Elvis
I like dance and music. I am artistic. I am very good at drawing.
Bogart
I am the strongest and the oldest pig. I always do whatever I want.
Audrey
I am a very good and caring pig. If someone cries, I cry with them. I never lie.
Milala
I think I am cute. I like to get attention from the other animals.
Goddard
I am very greedy. I like food.

The Story

One spring day, the Shorties were playing on a seesaw.

Aesop rushed over to them.

"That looks like so much fun, may I join you?" he asked.

"Of course," said the Shorties.

Aesop jumped onto the seesaw, and they all played together.

Presy saw Aesop playing on the seesaw.

"Aesop, don't you have to get ready for the play?"

Aesop stopped playing. "You're right Presy, let's get to work."

The Shorties wanted to stay on the seesaw.

"Okay, you all keep playing. Presy and I will get the play ready."

The Shorties kept playing on the seesaw.

"Is everything ready for the play?" Aesop asked Libbit.

"No, it is not!" said Libbit. "Can't you see the log is missing?"

Aesop looked onto the stage. "Where is the log? We need it for our play."

Libbit pointed to the field where the Shorties were playing on the seesaw.

"The Shorties have taken it and made it into a toy."

Bogart, the biggest of the Shorties, started jumping on the seesaw.

Just then, there was a loud snap.

The log broke in half.

"Oh no, what will we do without our log?" Aesop sighed deeply.

The Shorties were all surprised.

"Aesop," said the Shorties. "We are all very small. How could this have happened to a log that is so big?"

This gave Aesop a new idea for a play. He would call it *The Lion and the Mouse*.

One summer day, a lion was sleeping soundly.
Some mice ran over to try to scare him.
"You dare try to scare me? I am the strongest animal in the whole forest," said the lion.
The lion ran after the mice.
"I will eat the first mouse I catch!" roared the lion.
"Please spare us. We can help you someday," the mice squeaked as they ran away.
"Little mice help me?" the lion laughed.

The lion grew tired of chasing the mice.

"All right. I'll let you go if you promise to never scare me again."

The mice were very happy.

"Thank you for being so kind."

The mice squeaked as they bowed to the lion.

A few days later, the lion was looking for something to eat in the forest.

He saw a patch of mushrooms and ran over to eat them.

Before the lion could reach the mushrooms, he got caught in a trap. A net pulled the lion high into the air.

"Help me! Help me!" cried the lion.

The mice saw the lion caught in the net.

"Hang on! We will save you lion!" cried the smallest mouse.

All of the mice gnawed on the net with their teeth.

In the distance, the mice and the lion heard
the sound of a hunter. He was getting closer.
The lion and the mice were scared.
The mice tried to chew faster.
The net got tangled.
Aesop was stuck hanging in the air.
"Oh no!" cried Aesop. "Presy, stop the play!

The Shorties pulled on the ropes to try to free Aesop.

Aesop was still trapped. He was moving like a doll on strings.

Everyone watching started to laugh. They all thought it was part of the play.

"Everyone is enjoying it. Keep going!" said Aesop.

The Shorties kept pulling on the ropes.

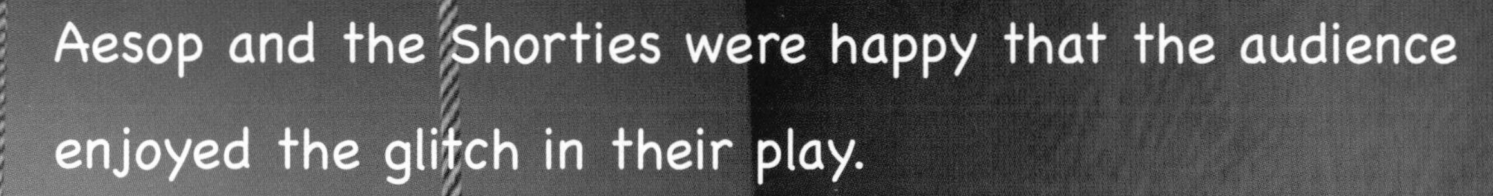

Aesop and the Shorties were happy that the audience enjoyed the glitch in their play.
Aesop smiled at the audience. The shorties bowed.
Everyone cheered for the actors.

Even little friends can be great friends.

What Is a Story?

Players

Who is the story about? The characters, or players, are the people, animals, or objects that perform the story. Characters have personality traits that contribute to the story. Readers understand how a character fits into the story by what the character says and does, what others say about the character, and how others treat the character.

Setting

Where and when do the events take place? The setting of a story helps readers visualize where and when the story is taking place. These details help to suggest the mood or atmosphere of the story. A setting is usually presented briefly, but it explains whether the story is taking place in the past, present, or future and in a large or small area.

Plot

What happens in the story? The plot is a story's plan of action. Most plots follow a pattern. They begin with an introduction and progress to the rising action of events. The events lead to a climax, which is the most exciting moment in the story. The resolution is the falling action of events. This section ties up loose ends so that readers are not left with unanswered questions. The story ends with a conclusion that brings the events to a close.

Point of View

Who is telling the story? The story is normally told from the point of view of the narrator, or storyteller. The narrator can be a main character or a less important character in the story. He or she can also be someone who is not in the story but is observing the action. This observer may be impartial or someone who knows the thoughts and feelings of the characters. A story can also be told from different points of view.

Dialogue

What type of conversation occurs in the story? Conversation, or dialogue, helps to show what is happening. It also gives information about the characters. The reader can discover what kinds of people they are by the words they say and how they say them. Writers use dialogue to make stories more interesting. In dialogue, writers imitate the way real people speak, so it is written differently than the rest of the story.

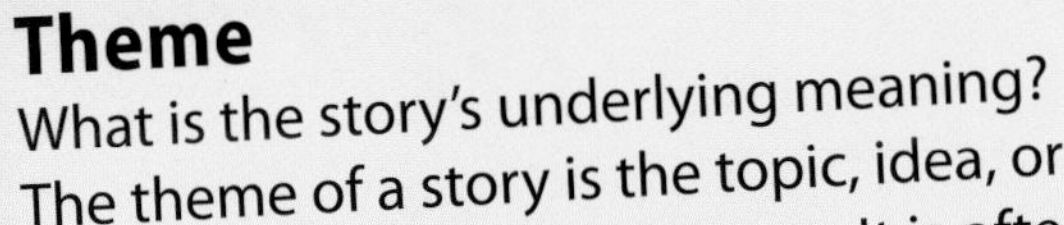

Theme

What is the story's underlying meaning? The theme of a story is the topic, idea, or position that the story presents. It is often a general statement about life. Sometimes, the theme is stated clearly. Other times, it is suggested through hints.

Quiz

1 What were Aesop and the Shorties playing on?

2 What did Presy ask Aesop to do?

3 What was Libbit missing from the stage?

4 Who broke the seesaw?

5 Why was the lion upset at the mice?

6 What did the lion try to eat in the forest?

Answers:

1. A seesaw
2. Prepare for the play
3. A log
4. Bogart
5. They tried to scare him.
6. Mushrooms

Key Words

Research has shown that as much as 65 percent of all written material published in English is made up of 300 words. These 300 words cannot be taught using pictures or learned by sounding them out. They must be recognized by sight. This book contains 120 common sight words to help young readers improve their reading fluency and comprehension. This book also teaches young readers several important content words, such as proper nouns. These words are paired with pictures to aid in learning and improve understanding.

Page	Sight Words First Appearance
4	a, also, am, an, and, be, been, but, can, have, I, man, of, plays, should, the, think, was
5	always, animals, at, do, food, from, get, good, if, like, never, other, them, to, very, want, with
7	all, asked, day, he, looks, may, much, on, one, over, said, so, story, that, they, together, were, you
8	don't, for, keep, right, saw, will, work
10	into, is, it, made, need, no, not, our, see, taken, we, where
12	are, big, call, could, how, idea, in, just, new, small, started, then, there, this, what, without, would
15	after, as, away, eat, first, help, him, little, me, some, try, us
17	again, being, go, kind, let
18	air, before, few, got, high, later, something
20	their
23	sound, stop
24	still
25	part, thought
27	great

Page	Content Words First Appearance
4	actor, leader, lion, manager, narrator, rabbit, screenwriter, theater
5	attention, dance, music, pig
7	seesaw
10	field, log, stage, toy
12	mouse, snap
15	forest
18	mushrooms, net, trap
20	teeth
23	hunter
24	doll, ropes, strings
27	audience, friends

Check out av2books.com for your animated storytime media enhanced book!

1. Go to av2books.com
2. Enter book code **H874671**
3. Fuel your imagination online!

www.av2books.com

AV² Storytime Navigation

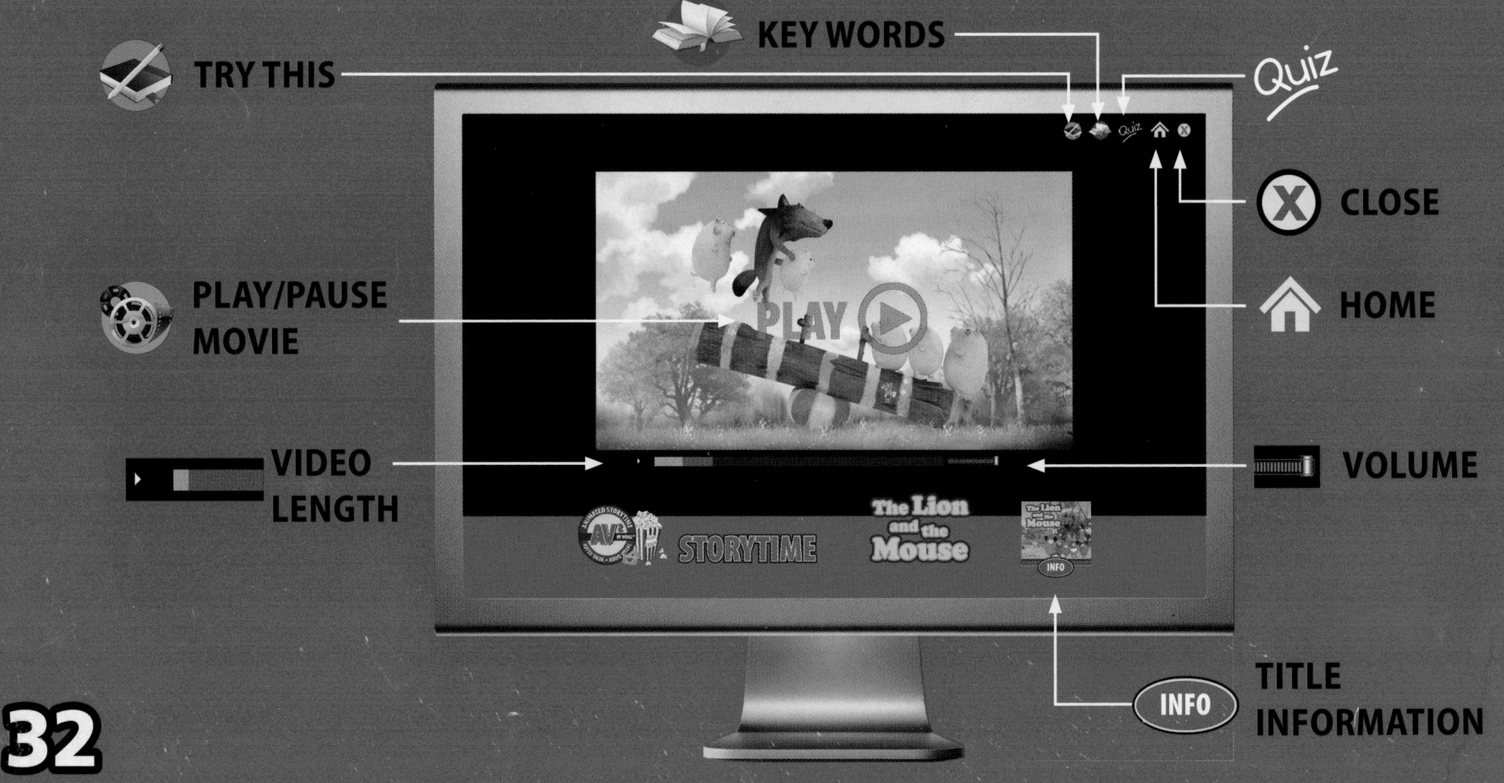